In Memory of
Horace W. French

WILD BILL HICKOK

MARYANN WEIDT

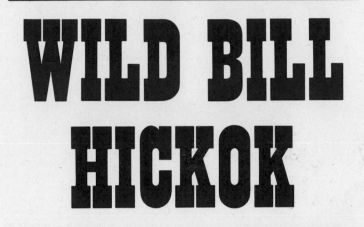

WILD BILL HICKOK

ILLUSTRATIONS BY STEVE CASINO

Lothrop, Lee & Shepard Books   **New York**

First Edition   1 2 3 4 5 6 7 8 9 10

Library of Congress Cataloging in Publication
Weidt, Maryann N. Wild Bill Hickok / by Maryann Weidt ; illustrated by Steve Casino.
    p.   cm. Summary: A fictional account of the life and adventures of the scout,
marshal, and showman known as Wild Bill Hickok. ISBN 0-688-10089-9. 1. Hickok, Wild
Bill, 1837–1876—Juvenile fiction. [1. Hickok, Wild Bill, 1837–1876—Fiction. 2. Frontier and
pioneer life—West (U.S.)—Fiction. 3. West (U.S.)—Fiction.] I. Casino, Steve, ill. II. Title.
PZ7.W42575W1 1992 [Fic]—dc20 92-9732 CIP AC

**To Alex David Weidt—
Without you my life would
be very dull.**

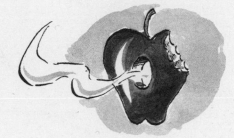

Contents

WILD BILL

HICKOK

Life in the
Old West

Life was tough in the Old West. To stay alive, you needed two things: a gun and a good horse. Most everybody carried a gun—men and women, sometimes even kids. Many a youngster learned to shoot a rifle and ride a pony as soon as he could walk. That's the way it was back then.

If you didn't have a gun, you couldn't hunt. And if you didn't hunt, you might not eat. The problem came when folks used a gun to settle a fight. That stopped the argument, all right. Most often, at least one person ended up dead. If the bullet didn't kill you right off, the doctoring might.

A good horse was the other thing you needed. Without a horse, you couldn't get out onto the prairie to hunt or go from one town to the next. There weren't all that many towns in the Old West. The ones that were there sat hundreds of miles apart.

To get from one place to another, you either rode your horse or caught the stagecoach. The stage didn't run too often, though. And riding in it for a day would make your backside ache for a week.

If you didn't take any food on the trip, you could eat at the stage stop. But you might not want to. Here's what was on the menu: pork, beans, hardtack, coffee, and whisky. If you couldn't eat pork, you were out of luck. If

you ate only beans, the other passengers were out of luck. If you ate only hardtack—biscuits that were as tough as boot leather—you might not have any teeth left to eat anything else.

But if you had a horse, you might not have to ride the stagecoach. Therefore, it was important to have a good horse. One of the worst crimes was stealing someone's horse. A horse thief, if he got caught, would be hanged. That was the law. Other than that, there weren't many laws in the Old West.

Sometimes folks in a town decided there was just too much killing going on. So they got together and elected a mayor. Then the mayor picked someone to be sheriff. Or, if the people were really well organized, they elected a sheriff, too. That's what happened to Wild Bill Hickok.

There were several reasons why Bill became sheriff. For one, he could shoot straight. For another, he did not tolerate a lot of rowdy behavior. So he became "the law" in a couple of towns in the Old West.

But that's not what Wild Bill Hickok started out to be. He didn't even start out with the name Bill.

The Real Wild Bill

Wild Bill's mama named him James Butler Hickok, after her father. James was born on May 27, 1837, on a farm half a mile from Little Vermilion Creek, near the town of Troy Grove, in northern Illinois. Troy Grove was called Homer at the time. James was the fourth son of William Alonzo Hickok and

Polly Butler Hickok. Two sisters came along later.

The Hickoks were kind-hearted farmers. They hated slavery. Some slaves ran away from their masters. The Hickoks hid them in a secret cellar underneath their living-room floor. Sometimes Mr. Hickok took the slaves to the next hiding place, at Panton's Mills. When this happened, James and his brothers rode along in the wagon. The boys huddled with the slaves under blankets and hay. None of them dared make a sound.

James learned to shoot a flintlock pistol when he was eight years old. He hunted gray wolves and sold their skins to earn spending money. James shot animals for his family to eat, too. He spent hours stalking the woods for rabbits, squirrels, and deer.

James liked to read almost as much as he liked to hunt. If nobody bothered him, he stayed in his attic room with his favorite books, *The Trapper's Guide* and *The Life of Kit Carson.*

When James was fifteen, his papa died. For a while, James helped his brothers work on the family farm. He helped out on other farms in the neighborhood, too. Then James and his brothers heard about the lush farmland for sale in Kansas. Folks said there was plentiful timber for building houses: walnut, hickory, oak, elm, willow, and cottonwood. The grasslands were rich with quail, prairie chickens, and wild turkeys. So, in June of 1856, James and his brother Lorenzo left Troy Grove to see for themselves.

For a time, James wrote letters to his family back in Illinois. But after a few years, he stopped. It seems he was too busy becoming a colorful character of the Old West. Reporters loved to write about him. They did not write about someone named James Butler Hickok, however. They wrote about a daredevil named "Wild Bill."

No one knows for sure how James came to be called Wild Bill. Some folks say that when he herded cattle in Nebraska Territory, his friends took to calling him "Duck Bill." That was before he had grown a paintbrush moustache to cover his top lip, which stuck out. Others claim his pals in the Civil War branded him Wild Bill because he was such a fearless scout.

From the beginning of the Civil War in 1861 until the end in 1865, Bill worked as a scout and a spy for the Union army. He sometimes carried messages between Springfield and Rolla, Missouri. On one of these trips, in the fall of 1863, he acquired a silky black mare that he named Black Nell.

It was said that when Bill whistled in a low tone, Nell would follow him up the steps of Ike Hoff's Saloon and climb up onto the pool table. Once, during the war, Confederate soldiers were chasing Bill. Nell saved his life by bounding over a wide stream and landing safely on the other side.

When Bill worked as a scout, he wore buckskin clothes and bright yellow moccasins. His moccasins weren't very big. Even

though he was tall—six feet and one inch—
he had small feet. Small hands, too.

Most gentlemen wore their hair short, but
not Bill. His long blond curls hung down to
his shoulders. His face looked like it had
been carved out of stone. He had steely blue-
gray eyes and his nose was a perfect triangle.

Wild Bill liked to wear expensive clothes.
No one knows for sure where he bought
them; maybe from a tailor in Kansas City.
When Bill got dressed up, he wore an em-
broidered vest. And when he got really
dressed up, he put on his Prince Albert frock
coat. This coat buttoned at the top and came
down to his knees. With it he wore black-
and-white-checked pants. He tucked the
pants into French calfskin boots so the
leather half-moon at the top would show.
Those boots alone must have cost Bill fifty
bucks worth of gold dust. The two-inch heels
made him even taller.

Sometimes Bill wore black velvet trousers
and tied a red silk sash around his waist. In it

he carried two pistols, whichever ones were his favorites at the time. His favorite hat was white and had a four-inch-wide brim.

Bill liked his fancy clothes. But there was one thing he liked more—a hot bath at the end of the day. At first, some of the cowboys laughed and teased him. But some of them gave it a try. Soon they, too, were visiting the bathhouse every day.

At the bathhouse in Deadwood, South Dakota, cowboys and miners—and anybody else who happened to be passing through town—could have a hot bath, a cold bath, or a shower bath. A hot bath cost about a quarter. A cold bath was cheaper, because the water had already been used by someone else.

Wild Bill liked to have fun, too. He could whistle and sing "Oh, Susanna!" and "Buffalo Gals." Sometimes he played his fiddle to entertain himself. Once in a while he got all dressed up in his fancy coat and went to a square dance. His long hair swung, and his

coat puffed out like a balloon, as he twirled the ladies round and round.

Like a lot of the fellows, Wild Bill enjoyed a good game of cards from time to time. He liked playing poker best of all. A lot of times he won. On the afternoon of August 2, 1876, Bill played his last game of cards. He was sitting in Saloon No. 10 in Deadwood, South Dakota. In his left hand he held two aces, two eights, and a jack. To this day, these cards are known as the "Dead Man's Hand."

But before Wild Bill died, he got himself into some mighty fine adventures. These next tales show just a few of the things that Wild Bill did. Most of what's written here is known fact. But some of it . . . Well, as one old-timer always said, "If these stories ain't true, they sure ought to be!"

Fighting the Cinnamon Bear

During 1859 and 1860, Wild Bill drove stagecoaches and freight wagons along the Santa Fe Trail between Independence, Missouri, and Santa Fe, New Mexico. He was twenty-two years old. The company he worked for was called Russell, Majors, and Waddell. They paid Bill about twenty dollars a month, plus all the hardtack and beans he could eat.

Some parts of the Santa Fe Trail wound along the Arkansas River and up into the Raton Mountains. One day in the fall of 1860, Bill was driving a freight wagon through the rockiest part of the trail, the Raton Pass. He was about two miles ahead of his partner, Matt Farley, going at a pretty good clip. Bill saw a clump of small pine trees up ahead. When he reached those trees, a big old cinnamon bear came lumbering out from behind them. She stopped in the middle of the trail and stood there. She had two cubs with her.

Bill screeched his wagon to a stop. He could see that this mama bear was not about to move. So he took off his hat and thought a minute. He should have thought for more than a minute. But he didn't. What Wild Bill decided to do was to take on that bear. Right then and there. He pulled out his gun. He aimed. He shot the bear square in the forehead.

Naturally, she got mad. And when she got mad, she wanted to fight. It was just as plain as the triangle nose on Bill's face—that bear was about to attack him. So Bill fired his gun again. This time he hit her in the left foreleg.

But did that stop the bear? Nope. It just made her madder. She jumped on Bill and threw him to the ground.

Bill wrestled that bear for close to an hour. Finally, he was too tired to move. He couldn't move anyway. The bear was on top of him. She was holding his left arm in her mouth, and she was not about to let go.

Just then Matt Farley, Bill's partner, came along. He thought Bill was dead, but he wasn't. It was the bear that was dead. Matt pried the bear's body off Wild Bill. Then he laid Bill in the wagon. He took him to Dr. Sam Jones's office in Santa Fe, seventy-five miles away. Dr. Jones was the best frontier surgeon around. He sewed Bill up.

Wild Bill rested for two months before he went back to Independence, Missouri. Many more months passed, however, before he was able to work again. Years passed before Bill forgot about that bear. In fact, he never really did forget about her. How could he? She had left scars on nearly every inch of his body.

The Law

Hays City, Kansas, became a town in the fall of 1867. It was the last stop on the Union Pacific Railroad. So when folks got to Hays City, they figured they might as well stay. Lots of different kinds of people ended up in Hays City, mostly because of the railroad. There were buffalo hunters, wagon-team drivers, soldiers, scouts, and, of course, the men who worked on the railroad.

When all those fellows finished work for the day, they wanted to have some fun. The truth was, there weren't many things you could do for fun in Hays City. You could drink whisky or you could gamble. Saloons and gambling houses sprang up like crocuses all over town.

By 1868, one resident counted twenty-two saloons and three dance halls. There was Hounddog Kelly's Saloon, Ed Goddard's Saloon and Dance Hall, and Paddy Walsh's Saloon and Gambling House, just to name a few on North Main Street. Soldiers from nearby Fort Hays liked to visit Tommy Drum's Saloon on Tenth Street. Also on North Main sat R. W. Evans' Grocery Store, Ol Cohen's Clothing Store, and the Perry Hotel.

The problem came about when the buffalo hunters, wagon-team drivers, soldiers, scouts, and railroad workers started drinking whisky in the saloons. The more whisky they drank, the more they started shootin' off their mouths. Once they started doing that, it wasn't long before they were shootin' off their guns at each other.

Wild Bill Hickok lived at the Perry Hotel in Hays City. He was tired of walking out every morning in his fancy frock coat and having to step over dead bodies in the streets. Plenty of other folks were fed up with all the killing, too. So, in August of 1869, they elected Bill sheriff of Ellis County, which included Hays City.

Bill decided right away to put a stop to all the shooting that was going on. So here's what he did. He had notices printed up. He went around and nailed them up all over town. The notices said it was against the law to carry a gun in town, much less fire one.

Of course, there was one bad guy who had to test the rule. His name was Bill Mulvey. He had been bullying his neighbors in St. Joseph, Missouri, for years. Now he went west looking to stir up more trouble. Mulvey

was not so bad when he hadn't been drinking. Whisky brought out the worst in him. And he liked to drink whisky.

It was the night of August 23 when Mulvey decided to challenge Wild Bill's rule. Mulvey had been drinking all day. Toward evening he boldly pulled out his guns. He started shooting his way down Front Street, hoping Wild Bill would come running. Sure enough, Wild Bill heard the commotion. He came around a corner, his long coattails flying. He found Mulvey with his guns drawn. Hickok told him he was under arrest for disturbing the peace. Mulvey growled, "I'm going to run you out of town, Wild Bill."

Wild Bill knew better than to try to argue with Mulvey. Instead, he outfoxed him. He turned and walked away. Mulvey snorted, thinking he really had run Wild Bill out of town. Then, suddenly, Wild Bill turned back. Mulvey was still facing him. Wild Bill looked over Mulvey's shoulder. He yelled, "Don't shoot him, boys. He's only fooling around!"

There was really nobody behind Mulvey, but he didn't know that.

It was the oldest trick in the book. But Mulvey wasn't too smart, and besides, he was pretty drunk. So he fell for it. He whipped around and looked behind him. As he did, Wild Bill shot him in the neck. That put an end to Bill Mulvey's bullying for good.

Wild Bill was a pretty strict sheriff. One old-timer said that Bill offered three choices to folks who did not obey his laws: (1) take the first eastbound train out of Hays; (2) take the first westbound train out of Hays; or (3) go north in the morning. "North" meant Boot Hill Cemetery.

Wild Bill served as sheriff of Hays City only until November of 1869. Then he was defeated by his deputy, Pete Lanahan. Bill lost by a vote of 114 to 89. He didn't mind. He was tired of trying to make everyone behave, and it was time to move on.

Bill decided to spend the winter in Topeka, Kansas, with his friend, Buffalo Bill Cody. No one is too sure what he did after that. But in April of 1871, Joseph McCoy, the mayor of Abilene, Kansas, sent for Wild Bill to become sheriff.

Abilene had been a nice, quiet little farming town of fewer than one thousand people—until the Texas cowboys started passing through. The trouble began when Mayor McCoy arranged a deal—all longhorn cattle heading north from Texas had to go through Abilene. He figured having all those cowboys in town would be good for business. What he hadn't figured was that it would be hard on law and order.

When the cowboys got to Abilene, they had been driving cattle for three months. They were ready to hoot and holler. They kept the bowling alley at Tom Downey's busy day and night. They played billiards at the Old Fruit. And at the Applejack, they gambled twenty-four hours a day. More than five thousand cowboys swarmed through Abilene during the summer of 1871.

When Bill became sheriff of Abilene, he again tried to enforce a law that there would be no shooting in the town. But it wasn't easy. Most of the cowboys carried guns. The farmers and the townsfolk had them, too.

Keeping the peace was especially tough on October 5, 1871. That was the day of the Dickinson County Fair. All the farmers in the area went to town for the fair. The cowboys, of course, were already there. The farmers tried to be nice to the cowboys. But, in truth, the farmers thought the cowboys and their cattle were ruining the peace and quiet of their little town.

By about nine o'clock that night, the cowboys and the farmers were getting on each other's nerves. Bill had a feeling there might be some trouble. So he asked his deputy, Mike Williams, to stand watch in front of the Novelty Theater. Bill strolled over to the Alamo Saloon.

Suddenly, a gambler named Philip Coe came out of the Bull's Head Saloon. He pulled out a gun and fired a shot in the air. Bill blasted through the doors of the Alamo with his guns drawn. Coe fired at Wild Bill. Bill shot back, putting two bullets in Coe's stomach. Just then, Deputy Williams darted across the street to see what was going on. Startled, Bill pulled the trigger and killed his own deputy.

Bill picked up his friend's limp body. He carried it into the Alamo Saloon and laid it on a poker table. Then he put his head down on the table and cried.

That was the last time Wild Bill ever pulled a gun on another man. He stayed in Abilene until the end of the year. Then he left town. The cowboys left, too, along with the cattle. Abilene went back to being a nice, quiet little town.

The Niagara Falls
Buffalo Hunt

In the spring of 1872, Wild Bill was on the move. This time he was headed north, to Niagara Falls, Canada. And he wasn't going alone. He was taking a few buffalo with him.

Here's what happened. Bill met a man named Sidney Barnett in Kansas City. Colonel Barnett had heard all about Wild Bill. So he hired him to put together a Wild West show. The show would be called "The Niagara Falls Buffalo Hunt." It would begin July 1 and run through the Fourth of July.

Bill didn't know that much about buffalo. He had never roped a buffalo in his life. But he thought, "How hard could it be?" He soon found out.

Bill hired three cowboys to help him. They rode north along the Republican River. They followed the river across the border into Nebraska. Finally, when they came to Beaver Creek, Nebraska, they found some buffalo. Now they had to rope them. Bill tried first. He made the loop of his lasso too big. The loop slipped over the animal's hump. The buffalo pulled, and the rope went tight. Bill hung on and over he flew. His face hit the ground like a rock. He was lucky he didn't smash his perfect triangle nose. He did, however, pick prairie grass out of his teeth for a week.

After several tries, Bill and the cowboys captured six buffalo. Then came the really hard part: getting the buffalo to move in the direction the men wanted them to go. The men pushed. They pulled. They shoved and tugged. Finally, they dragged the animals across the prairie. It took the four men two weeks to get six buffalo from Beaver Creek to Ogallala, Nebraska.

At Ogallala, Bill hired four Comanche Indians to go along and be part of the show. He put the buffalo on the Union Pacific train to Omaha and then to Niagara Falls. He and the Comanches and the cowboys boarded the train, too. Before long, they were all in Niagara Falls.

Every year, thousands of tourists visited the spectacular Niagara waterfalls. Bill figured he and Colonel Barnett would put together a show that would be a bigger splash than the falls itself. Unfortunately, there were problems too numerous to mention. The show could not go on as planned. It was postponed until later in the summer, August 28 and 30, to be exact.

An ad for the show in the *Niagara Falls* (New York) *Gazette* read: "This novel and most exciting affair will positively take place on the days mentioned and will be under the management and direction of 'Wild Bill' (Mr. William Hickok), the most celebrated Scout and Hunter of the Plains."

On the first day of "The Niagara Falls Buffalo Hunt," nearly five thousand people turned out. But there was no place for them to sit. Bill had forgotten to set up bleachers. The audience milled about. The folks in the front could see six buffalo inside a wire fence. The ones in the back could see only the people in front of them.

Bill shot off his gun to start the show. The noise startled the buffalo. They bolted from the pen and ran off through the streets. Now, that was exciting. All the kids in the crowd— and some grown-ups, too—chased after the buffalo. Meanwhile, a trained cinnamon bear got loose and attacked a sausage vendor. Nobody's sure whether the bear was after the

vendor or the sausages. Not many folks stayed around to find out. As it turned out, the bear ate the sausages and the vendor ran for his life.

Bill, meanwhile, quickly passed the hat to everyone who was still around. He came up with $123.86. It was enough to buy four train tickets for the Comanches to get back to Nebraska. He sold the buffalo to the local butchers. Buffalo burgers were a popular item at the Niagara Falls restaurants that week. Bill and the cowboys rode the freight trains back to Kansas City.

Hot Shot

Some of the tales about Wild Bill's know-how with a gun seem a bit farfetched. Old-timers vow they saw him shoot the bottom right out of a bottle without breaking the neck. Some folks swear that Bill could drive a cork through the neck of a bottle with a bullet. Others claim that he could even shoot a hole through a dime at fifty paces.

Dr. Joshua Thorne of Kansas City once bet Wild Bill five dollars that he could not cut a rooster's throat with a bullet without breaking its neck. Bill was sometimes as cocky as a rooster himself. He strutted around and said he was sure he could do it. The gun he carried at the time was a .41-caliber derringer. Bill picked out a rooster about twenty-five yards away and pulled the trigger. The rooster's blood splattered, but its neck was not broken. Bill went home five dollars richer. He might even have gotten to keep the rooster.

The people of Hays City remember a time Bill was walking down the streets of their town. He spied a ripe apple hanging from a tree. He thought it might be fun to make applesauce. He pulled out both his guns. With one bullet he cut the stem. The apple fell. Before it hit the ground, he put a hole smack through it with his other pistol.

To this day, the folks down in Abilene tell

tales about Bill when he was sheriff of their city. One story goes like this: One day two men murdered another man. Bill hurried to the saloon where the shooting had taken place. The two gunmen were still there. However, just as Bill came in the front door, the murderers left through the back door. Bill followed them. He stepped outside. He looked left and saw one man running in that direction. He looked right and saw the other one headed that way. Bill took out his guns. He fired both right and left at the same time. He killed both men. A young boy was on his way to school and heard the noise. He told the coroner that Wild Bill had killed two men with a single bullet. Bill had fired his guns at exactly the same time, so it sounded like one shot.

Some folks claim they saw Wild Bill in 1873 or 1874 on tour with Buffalo Bill Cody's Prairie Waif Company. They played for three days in Milwaukee. One night Bill took some of the boys to the outskirts of town to show

off how well he could shoot. First he placed two solid bricks about two feet apart on top of a fence. Then he stood back about fifteen yards. He aimed one pistol at each brick. He pulled the triggers and both bricks broke in half. Again, the shots were fired so close together that they sounded like one.

Then Bill threw a quart can ten to twelve feet in front of him. He pulled out both guns and began firing so fast at the ground that the can bounced along like a jumping bean as Bill walked toward it. It was kind of like playing kick the can, only with guns. Bill kept shooting, first with his right hand, then with his left, until his guns were empty.

The guns Bill used beginning in 1869 were silver-plated Colt .44s with white pearl handles. The story goes that Senator Henry Wilson gave Bill those guns as a gift for escorting him and a group of his friends on a tour of the West. Senator Wilson was active in the antislavery movement and wrote several books on the subject. He was elected Vice

President of the United States in 1872. Nobody knows for sure whether Bill led the tour or not. What is certain is that Bill carried the pearl-handled guns to his dying day.

The Scouts of the
Plains Hit
New York City

Buffalo Bill Cody invited Wild Bill Hickok
to come to New York City in the fall of 1873.
Cody and his friends were putting on plays
about the Wild West. Cody invited Wild Bill
to stay with him at the Metropolitan Hotel. He
told him to catch a cab at the depot. He
warned him that the cab driver might try to

overcharge him. But no matter what he says, cautioned Cody, do not pay him more than two dollars.

Cody thought he could make Hickok a star. When Wild Bill arrived at the Forty-second Street Depot, he was dressed like a star. He was wearing his Prince Albert coat with a red flowered vest, a ruffled white shirt, and a string tie. He had on black-and-white-checked pants, his high-heeled boots, and a broad-brimmed hat.

Wild Bill followed his friend's instructions. He got into a horse-drawn cab. He told the driver to take him to the hotel. Sure enough, when they arrived, the driver told him the fare was five dollars. Wild Bill complained. The driver jumped down from his seat. He aimed his fists at Wild Bill. But before that driver knew what hit him, he was lying face down in the street.

The hotel manager saw all the excitement. He ran to Buffalo Bill's room and told him that the man he had been expecting had arrived.

Making Hickok a star turned out to be a tougher job than Buffalo Bill had imagined. Wild Bill had a strong voice, and he was handsome. But when he set foot on a theater stage, he felt like a fool. The problem was he refused to follow the script. Or maybe he couldn't remember his lines. But he always wound up saying just about anything that came into his head. Sometimes the audience loved it. Other times they booed him right off the stage.

Wild Bill also had trouble with the lights. Years of being outside in the bright prairie sun had hurt his eyes. He couldn't stand being in the spotlight. He waved it away so much that the audience thought it was part of the show. Sometimes they took off their hats and waved back at him.

The first performance of *Scouts of the Plains* was at Niblo's Gardens in New York City. Wild Bill did everything he could to avoid the spotlight. He even hid behind some scenery. But the light kept following him. Finally, Bill pulled out his pistol. But he

didn't shoot that light. He threw the pistol at it. Bull's-eye! The audience whooped and shouted. Wild Bill took a bow. Buffalo Bill, however, was not pleased.

After a time, Wild Bill grew tired of trying to be an actor. On March 10, 1874, during a performance at the Rochester (New York) Opera House, he told Buffalo Bill's wife that he was done making a fool of himself. After the show, Wild Bill packed his bags and headed west.

The Dead Man's Hand

It was shortly after noon on Wednesday, August 2, 1876. Bill sat in Nuttall and Mann's Saloon No. 10 in Deadwood, South Dakota. It was almost too hot to wear a Prince Albert coat, but Bill was wearing it anyway, with his black-and-white-checked pants. He was playing poker with his pals Captain Massie, Carl Mann, and Charlie Rich.

Bill usually sat with his back to the wall so nobody could sneak up on him. But not this time. He had asked Charlie to trade places with him, but Charlie had refused. He said he didn't want to be bothered with any of Bill's silly superstitions. Wild Bill should have insisted.

Bill was used to winning at poker. The night before, in fact, he had beaten Captain Massie pretty heavily. But today Bill was losing to Massie. He would be lucky if he didn't lose his clean, white shirt.

Finally Bill drew a decent hand of cards, two pair: aces and eights. It was the best hand he'd had all day.

About three o'clock, the door of Saloon No. 10 swung open and in walked Jack "Crooked Nose" McCall. Jack was short and built like a bull. He moved his large head from side to side. His tiny black eyes peered around the room. He pulled his wide sombrero down to hide his ugly face.

Bill was so intent on his cards that he did not even notice Jack. Suddenly Bill felt something cold and hard on the back of his head. He heard the words "Take that!" as the sound of a gunshot echoed through the room. Bill slumped forward and fell to the floor. The cards he had been holding in his left hand dropped to the floor, too. They were the ace of spades, the ace of clubs, two black eights, and the jack of diamonds—the "Dead Man's Hand."

Jack McCall stood holding a smoking .45-caliber pistol. He pointed the gun at the other people in the saloon and glared at them. They all ran out the front door. Jack turned and headed for the back door, into the dusty Deadwood sun. He grabbed a horse. He didn't care who owned it. He took hold of the reins and the saddle horn. He threw his leg up and over. But the owner had loosened the saddle to help the horse stay cool. The saddle slipped and Jack landed in the dirt. He stood up and shook himself off.

Then Jack took off down the street. He ducked into Jacob Shroudy's Butcher Shop and tried to hide behind the counter. Saloon-keeper Ike Brown and some of the boys found Jack and took it upon themselves to arrest him. There was no sheriff in town at the time and no judge either. So a meeting was called to decide what to do. The citizens of Deadwood selected twelve men to serve as the jury. They chose Colonel May as the prosecuting attorney. It was his job to try to prove McCall was guilty of the murder of Wild Bill. Joseph Miller was chosen to defend McCall.

The trial began at nine o'clock the next day at McDaniels' Theater. Most everyone in town came to watch. Jack said he had an excuse for killing Wild Bill. He said he was just getting even for Bill's killing his brother down in Kansas. The jury believed Jack, despite his surly appearance. The law of the Old West was "a life for a life." If Bill had killed Jack's brother, then Jack was right to gun down Wild Bill.

The jury came back with this verdict: "Deadwood City, August 3rd, 1876. We, the jury, find Mr. John McCall not guilty." McCall walked out of that room a free man. He stayed in Deadwood a few days. Then he saddled up his own skinny horse. He made sure the saddle was tight. He headed for Julesburg, Colorado, and hired on as a ranch hand. It was harvest time, so there was plenty of work to do.

After the men had been hoeing in the hot sun for a few days, the rancher thought they deserved a reward. He had his cooks prepare a banquet. He brought out his best whisky. The men ate and drank far into the night.

The next day, Jack did not show up for work. Some of the men told the boss that he had left for good. What was more, he had taken off with most of the leftover food from the party. As if that was not enough, he had made off with his boss's best horse and saddle.

Jack rode toward Wyoming. Along the way, he told everybody he met that he had killed Wild Bill Hickok. He bragged that he had gotten away with it, too. He said he had lied about Wild Bill's killing his brother.

Jack should have kept his mouth shut. In Wyoming, federal marshals arrested him. They took him to Yankton, South Dakota, because it was the capital of the territory. There he was put on trial again. Now he admitted he had lied about Wild Bill's killing his brother. One witness said Jack didn't even have a brother. The jury found him guilty of the murder of Wild Bill Hickok.

On March 1, 1877, Jack McCall was hanged for the murder of Wild Bill Hickok. Some people say he was buried with a piece of rope still clinging to his neck.

Wild Bill's body lies buried in Mount Moriah Cemetery in Deadwood, South Dakota. He took to his grave the clothes he had loved the most—the Prince Albert coat, a boiled white shirt, and black-and-white-checked trousers. Some who saw him said his long blond hair looked as pretty in death as it had when he was alive. Wild Bill's family found out about his death several months after it happened. They read about it in the newspaper.

Maryann Weidt

was born in Minnesota, where she grew up on a small dairy farm. An only child, she constantly read and made up stories, many of them about cowboys and the West. The very best gift she ever got was a cowgirl outfit, complete with hat and holsters.

Maryann was a children's librarian for twenty years and is also the author of *Presenting Judy Blume*. She now lives in Duluth, Minnesota, with her husband and their son and daughter.

Steve Casino

was born in Jeannette, Pennsylvania, and grew up in a very small town near the Ohio border. His favorite childhood interests were science and nature, and he especially enjoyed making pets of bees. Steve has worked as an advertising prop and model maker, designed toys, and illustrated magazines and comic books. He lives in Hoboken, New Jersey.